P9-CQE-833

Rabén & Sjögren Bokförlag, Stockholm
www.raben.se

Translation copyright © 2005 by Rabén & Sjögren Bokförlag
Originally published in Sweden by Eriksson & Lindgren under the title *Malla cyklar*
Copyright © 2003 by Eva Eriksson
Library of Congress Control Number: 2003098292
Printed by Narayana Press, Gylling, Denmark
First American edition, 2005
ISBN 91-29-66156-0

EVA ERIKSSON

A CRASH COURSE
FOR MOLLY

Translated by Elisabeth Kallick Dyssegaard

R&S
BOOKS

Stockholm   New York   London   Adelaide   Toronto

Molly is big and smart.
Now she can ride a bike.

Oops!

She really *can* ride her bike.

She rides every day.
It's her favorite thing to do.

And she rides fast.
"Don't ride so fast!" yells Grandma.
"Watch out for the pole!"

The pole? Why would she hit it?
It's right in the middle of the path. Molly looks at the
pole. Just to be on the safe side, she
looks at it the whole time. She rides closer . . .

. . . and closer . . .

Crash! She hits the pole!

"Why did you hit the pole?" asks Grandma.
"I told you to watch out!"
It *is* strange.

Luckily, Molly only hurt herself in the place where she
already has a Band-Aid.
The bicycle is all in one piece, too. So they can easily keep going.
In the distance the driving instructor is taking a walk.
"Now, don't hit the driving instructor," jokes Grandma.
Molly laughs. The driving instructor is far away on the
other side of the path.

To be on the safe side, she looks at him
the whole time so
that she won't hit him by mistake.
She gets closer . . .

. . . and closer . . .

Crash! Now she's hit the driving instructor as well.

This is terrible! What has she done?
Grandma is upset, too.

But the driving instructor takes it pretty well.
He's been in worse crashes.
With CARS!
"I don't understand why she has to ride into everything,"
says Grandma. "She doesn't look where she's going!"
Molly is crying.
"I was looking! I looked at the driving instructor the whole
time. And I still crashed!"

"Aha!" says the driving instructor. "There's the explanation. That's exactly what you are not supposed to do. If you meet a truck on the road, you should not look at it. You should look ahead to where you are going. If you look at something too long, you may turn the steering wheel in that direction, and, bang, you crash. You have to look straight ahead at the road. Then you'll drive straight and well."

Grandma and the driving instructor stand facing each
other. Now Molly has to practice not hitting them.
"Look ahead to where you are going and not at us!"

Molly rides back and forth between them. She looks straight ahead. She does well. She doesn't crash even once.

"How lucky that we met such a nice driving instructor,"
says Grandma. She wonders whether she should start taking
driving lessons.
"Do you think I'm too old to learn to drive a car?"
"It's never too late," says the driving instructor.

On the way back, there are some kids that Molly has to avoid
hitting. She looks straight ahead. She comes closer.
Now they are yelling something, something mean.

Are they yelling at her?
She'll have to look at them.
She looks . . .

. . . and looks. Help, she's looking!
What now? Is she going to hit them, too?

No!
Because Molly rides really well now. She has just taken a
bike-riding lesson.

She can bike even better than Grandma!

Who would have thought!